I'll do better," said Matthew. "You'll see."

Matthew's eyes widened. He couldn't believe it. Written at the top of the extra page were six words: "Math Test Six. Mr. Johnson's Class."

Matthew was holding the test his class would take on Friday. But this test was different. It had the answers on it.

KARATE KIDS
Grounded for Life?

by **Alex Simmons**
illustrated by
Alan Tiegreen

created by
Steve DeMasco

TABLE OF CONTENTS

MEET THE KIDS
OF THE
COOL KARATE SCHOOL

Matthew "Snake" Davis
The Snake is quick and smooth. Being too smooth sometimes gets Matthew in trouble. He started studying karate to learn how to fight. Now he's learning a lot more than that.

Marissa "Dragon" Santos
The Dragon has fighting spirit. And so does Marissa. She says you have to have a fighting spirit with four older brothers. Not to mention a group of pushy friends.

Jonathan "Tiger" Scott
In karate, the Tiger stands for strength. In Jonathan's case, it also stands for stubborn and spoiled. Now Jonathan is learning that some things are more important than his parents' money.

Susan "Leopard" Ziegler
Fast and powerful, that's the Leopard. And so is Susan. Sometimes the leopard is angry—and so is Susan. The kids try to help, but she doesn't make it easy.

Willy "Crane" Ray
The Crane stands for grace and balance. Willy is tall and slim, like the crane. He's working on the grace and balance. He has to learn fast because his father is always pushing him to win.

CHAPTER

THE TROUBLE WITH MATH

"How much is one fourth of 48?" Marissa Santos asked.

"Give me a break!" said Matthew Davis. They were at karate school. He did a forward roll and jumped up. Matthew was nine and a half. His black hair was cut flat on the top and short at the back and sides.

"Come on!" Marissa shook her head. "That problem is easy. We did it in class today."

"And Mr. Johnson called on me because he knew I didn't know the answer," Matthew said. "He wanted me to look bad."

"I think you're taking this too personally," said Willy Lee Ray. He ruffled his light-brown hair.

1

"Well, you're wrong," Matthew said. He began doing deep knee bends. "Mr. Johnson has it in for me. And I want to get even."

"The camera zooms in for a tight close-up," said Jonathan Scott. "Our hero vows to get even with his archenemy, *Dr. Mad Math*."

"Remind me to laugh," Matthew said.

"What are you going to do?" Susan Ziegler asked. She was sitting on the floor doing stretches. "Attack Mr. Johnson on the street at night and force him to up your grades?"

"What's the point of learning karate if I don't use it?" Matthew grinned.

He and his friends were students at the Grecco School of Karate. They liked the school so much they called it the Cool Karate School.

They practiced in a big room with safety mats on the floor. One wall was covered with mirrors. The other walls were decorated with Asian symbols and pictures. The place felt like a real *dojo*, the Japanese word for "school."

The dojo was run by Tommy and Su Grecco.

Tommy and Su were married. They'd met in Vietnam, Su's homeland, when Tommy was in the U.S. army.

"We're not here to bash people," Jonathan said. "Tommy and Su are always reminding us karate is not about force."

"I know that," Matthew said. "But this is different!"

Marissa rolled her eyes. She was nine years old. She had dark-brown hair and skin the color of almonds. "You're mad at Mr. Johnson because he doesn't believe your lame excuses."

"You wouldn't have a problem if you did better on your tests," Susan said.

"Mr. Johnson's tests aren't fair!" Matthew said. He made fists and raised his arms. He looked tough, he thought.

"What's wrong with them?" Willy asked. He was walking on his hands.

"Matthew has to do the problems." Marissa laughed.

"Real funny," Matthew said.

3

"If I were a teacher, I'd be angry at you too," Marissa said.

"Why was he angry?" Jonathan asked. He and Willy went to a different school from Matthew, Marissa, and Susan.

"I didn't hand in my homework," said Matthew.

"He told Mr. Johnson it fell into the chili he was helping his mom cook!" said Marissa.

Everyone but Matthew laughed.

"You guys don't understand. Mr. Johnson is giving a math test on Friday. I have to —"

Tommy and Su walked into the room. "Line up for class," Tommy said.

Jonathan put his arm around Matthew's shoulders. "Tune in tomorrow for more of *The Young and the Mathless!*"

Marissa laughed, and Matthew chased her across the room.

The five friends joined the other students. They formed three rows in front of Tommy and Su. All the students wore white baggy uniforms called *gis* ("gees").

The jackets had no buttons. They were held closed by cloth belts. The belts came in different colors. Each color showed how good a person was at karate. Matthew and his friends were all blue belts. That was the second level.

Willy poked Matthew in the back. "There are five kids in each row. There are three rows. How many kids are in the class?"

"Chill," Matthew whispered. "I can count."

"Is something wrong?" Su asked Matthew.

"No, *sensei*," Matthew replied. "Everything is fine." *Sensei* ("sen-say") is the Japanese word for teacher.

Su looked small standing next to Tommy. He was very strong. But he was always gentle with the children.

"**Preparation positions, please,**" Su said. Preparation was the special time before they started practicing.

Matthew and the others sat on the floor. He closed his eyes and crossed his legs. Then he took deep breaths and let them out slowly.

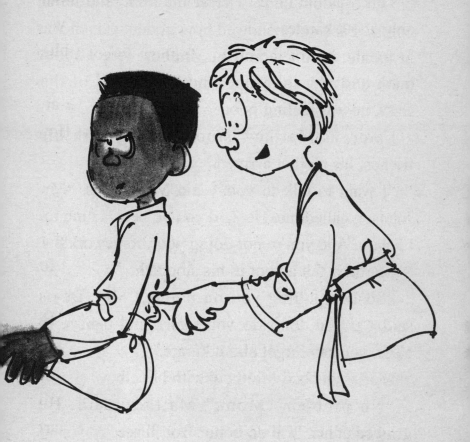

In and out, in and out.

This was the time to clear his mind and think only about karate.

For the rest of the class, Matthew forgot about math and Mr. Johnson. And by the end of the class, he was feeling good.

Later, as Matthew stood talking with his friends, his mother arrived.

"I want to talk to you," said Mrs. Davis. "Mr. Johnson called me. He said you've been acting up in class. And you're not doing your homework."

Matthew felt a knot in his stomach.

"So I'm putting you on notice," Mrs. Davis said. "If you don't do your work and behave in class, you can forget about karate."

Marissa jabbed Matthew with her elbow.

"No problem, Mom," Matthew said. He grinned at her. "I'll do better. You'll see."

GOOD AS GOLD

"Making rude noises is not funny," said Mr. Johnson the next day in class.

Matthew grinned. He'd had fun grunting like a pig. And the kids had been giggling. That was cool.

Mr. Johnson took off his glasses. "Do you think the principal will find your actions funny—this time?"

A chorus of *Ooooooooooo*'s filled the room. Matthew stopped grinning.

"No, sir," he said.

Being sent to Mr. Polanski's office was definitely not a good thing. You didn't fool around with Mr. P.

Mr. Polanski was a big man with a deep voice. *If he ever smiles, it must be in a dark closet in the middle of the night,* Matthew thought. His parents had met with Mr. Polanski. More than once. It had not been fun.

"You already have some minus points to work off," said Mr. Johnson. "And we have a math test Friday."

"I know," Matthew said. He looked around the classroom. Most of the kids were still smiling. Marissa was in the row next to him. She looked angry.

"This class has been misbehaving all afternoon. I will not stand for any more—from anyone."

Matthew sat up in his seat. Then he shrugged. He didn't want to anger Mr. Johnson anymore. But he didn't want to look uncool either.

Mr. Johnson turned to the chalkboard. The class was studying current events.

Matthew liked this subject, but he didn't want to show it.

"Do that pig noise again," said Trina. She sat

behind Matthew. Matthew shook his head. "Come on," she whispered. "What are you, chick-en?"

Matthew gave her a dirty look. He glanced back at Mr. Johnson. He was still writing on the chalk-board.

Marissa reached across the aisle and hit Matthew on the arm.

"Don't you dare," she whispered. "You get in trouble, and your mom will pull you out of karate class."

"Go on, Matthew," Trina said. "Do it again."

Marissa gave her a cold stare. Trina sat back in her seat.

"I won't get in trouble," Matthew whispered. "I've got it under control."

Marissa's eyes flashed. "You always think that. Then you—"

Mr. Johnson turned around. "That's it! Marissa, you may visit the principal."

"But I—"

"I do not want to hear any excuses."

Mr. Johnson began writing out a pass.

Matthew spoke up. "I was the one talking. Marissa was trying to get me to be quiet." Matthew couldn't believe he was doing this.

Marissa glanced at Matthew, then back at Mr. Johnson.

Mr. Johnson studied Matthew for a long moment.

"Have a nice visit, Matthew," he said. "And give Mr. Polanski my regards."

Matthew walked to the front of the room. He took the pass. Everyone was watching. He shrugged, then walked out the door as if he didn't care.

But once he was in the hallway, his shoulders sagged. *In trouble again,* he thought. *Just great.* He went downstairs.

"Here again, Matthew?" Mrs. Rodney asked. She was the principal's secretary. Her blue-gray hair was puffed out like cotton candy.

"Yeah," Matthew said.

"Mr. Polanski is in a meeting, but he'll be free

soon," Mrs. Rodney said. "Make yourself useful." She handed him three sheets of paper. "Please take these to the copy room. Ask Mr. Doyle to make me two copies of each letter, right away."

Matthew took the papers. He walked to a little room down the hall.

In one corner was a photocopy machine. Next to it was a short, nervous man.

"Hi, Mr. Doyle," Matthew said. Mr. Doyle grumbled hello. He was copying a stack of paper.

"Mrs. Rodney says she needs two copies of these."

"I suppose she needs them right away," Mr. Doyle said.

Matthew nodded. Mr. Doyle slapped down his stack of paper, took Matthew's pages, and made the copies.

"There you are," he said. He handed the papers to Matthew. "Now run along. I have tons of work to do."

Matthew straightened out the papers Mr. Doyle had given him. He had seven pages instead of six.

Matthew's eyes widened. He couldn't believe it.

Written at the top of the extra page were six words: "Math Test Six. Mr. Johnson's Class."

Matthew was holding the test his class would take on Friday. But this test was different. It had the answers on it.

CHAPTER

IT'S NOT EASY
BEING A KID

"This is one hundred percent gold!" Matthew whispered. He stared at the test. *If I use this, I'll ace the test Friday*, he said to himself.

But it would be cheating. He could imagine what his parents would say if they found out.

"I thought I taught you to stand on your own two feet," his father would say.

"I'm very angry about what you did," his mother would say. Then they'd seal him up in his room for the rest of his life.

Matthew imagined himself trapped in the dark. Thick bars were on the window. He was wearing an iron mask. The words "Family Cheat" were on the front of it.

Was it worth taking the chance?

He folded the paper and slipped it into his pocket.

I have a lot to figure out, Matthew thought. *Maybe the gang at the dojo can help me.*

"Yeah," he whispered. "They're my friends, and we can talk about anything. I'll show it to them tomorrow. I bet they can tell me what to do."

"Get away from me!" Marissa turned her back on Matthew. "I don't want to hear any more!"

Willy and Jonathan laughed.

"How can you be such a jerk?" Susan asked.

"What's wrong with you guys?" Matthew asked. "It's not like I tattooed your dogs or something."

"I don't have a dog," Jonathan said.

"What I meant was—"

"It doesn't matter," Marissa said. "It still stinks!"

"Why are you so bent out of shape?" Matthew asked.

17

"I work for my grades!" Marissa said. "I study hard, and I do my homework—by myself."

"Not all the time," Susan said.

Marissa looked embarrassed. "Okay. So you helped me with one of my assignments."

"One?" Susan asked.

"All right. Maybe you helped me with a couple, but—"

"A couple?"

"So you help me a lot." The gang laughed.

"But she helps me do my *own* work."

"I'll be doing my own work," Matthew said.

Susan snickered. "Copying the answers isn't work!"

"Look, Matthew," said Willy. "If you get caught, you'll be in a lot of trouble."

"I won't get caught!"

"And a rattler won't hiss beneath a cold, cold rock," Willy replied.

Everyone stared at him.

"What's that supposed to mean?" Jonathan asked.

Willy shrugged. "I don't know. It's something my grandma used to say. And Matthew's karate name is Snake."

Matthew shook his head. "What I mean is—"

"Did you have rattlesnakes where you lived?" Marissa asked.

Willy nodded.

"Did they hiss?"

Willy looked confused. "They mostly rattled."

Matthew tried again. "If I use the test answers—"

"Then why did your grandmother say something so weird?" Susan asked.

"She always said stuff like that," Willy replied.

Matthew threw up his hands. "What about the test answers?"

Susan moved close to him. "We're your friends, right?"

Matthew nodded.

"And we all stick together, right?" Susan asked.

"That's the code of our club," Matthew said. "Snake, Crane, Leopard, Tiger, and Dragon.

20

Together as one, just like in karate."

"Good," Susan said. "Then the answer is simple." She stepped closer. "If you use that answer sheet, we'll brain you."

"You don't understand. My mom is going to make me quit karate if I don't do better in school." He looked around. "I've got to use those answers."

"That's real smart!" Marissa said.

Matthew's eyes narrowed. "Like none of you has ever cheated!"

"I never had the nerve," Willy said.

"I've never needed to," Susan said.

"I did," Jonathan said. "Back in private school."

"I knew it!" Matthew grinned at them. "So what happened?" he asked.

Jonathan shrugged. "I'm not in that school anymore. And my parents took away my privileges for months."

"I never cheated on anything in my life," Marissa declared. Everyone stared at her. "Well... only on my diets."

"All right, kids. It's time," Tommy called from

the center of the room.

"We're not perfect little angels," Susan said. "But we all agree on this. Using that answer sheet is dumb."

Matthew lowered his head. "Dumb is how I feel in class. What's the difference?"

"Oh, forget it!" Marissa stormed off.

Jonathan and Susan followed her.

Willy ran his hand through his hair. "Think about it," he said. "Okay?"

"Okay," Matthew said.

Whoever said being a kid was easy didn't have a clue.

CHAPTER 4

BAD NEWS

Tommy and the students bowed to one another. Bowing was part of the karate tradition. It was a way to show respect to your teacher and to yourself.

When he first started karate, Matthew thought bowing was weird. Now it seemed perfectly normal. Even a little cool.

"Positions for preparation," Tommy said.

"Sensei, where is Su?" Willy called out.

"Su is unable to join us today," Tommy said.

"What's wrong?" Matthew asked.

"She . . . Su had some bad news today. It upset her. She needs to be alone to think."

"Sometimes I get really bad news," said Blair

Thomas. She was one of the older students. Her hair was cut short except for a long strand that hung down over her right eye. "Like, I mean true bummer," she said. "I put on my Platinum Yo Yo tapes and, like, blast the blues away."

Tommy smiled. "I'll suggest that to Su."

"Is Su going to be all right?" Marissa asked.

"I'm sure she will," Tommy said.

He held up his hands. "Thank you for your concern. But let's focus on karate."

Everyone became quiet. Matthew had never heard his *sensei* sound so sad before.

He glanced at his friends. Like him, they were worried. Su had never missed a class.

The students sat down.

But Matthew couldn't focus. When he closed his eyes, all he could see was the answer sheet.

Why should something so simple be a problem? Use the answers and pass the test. Don't use them and fail. What should he do?

Focus time ended. The lesson began.

Matthew tried to concentrate. The class did

warm-ups. Then they practiced their forms. Forms were karate movements everyone did at the same time.

Some moves were strong and fast, like a tiger. Others were slow and smooth, like a snake.

For a while, Matthew forgot about everything but karate. Even the math test slipped from his mind.

Until they started to practice the roundhouse kick. It was a difficult move. Matthew spun around on one leg and kicked with the other. But he wasn't quick and smooth.

"I can't get it!" Matthew shouted.

"Everything takes practice," Tommy said. "We have to work hard to get what we want."

"Will I get what I want if I work hard?" Matthew asked.

Tommy looked as he had when the class had asked about Su.

"Not always," Tommy said.

"Then why bother?"

"The fact that you tried means a lot," Tommy said.

Tommy demonstrated the roundhouse kick slowly to show the whole class.

The kids eagerly watched every move. But Matthew was thinking about what Tommy had *said*.

If Tommy didn't believe hard work was the answer, why should he?

The class practiced the roundhouse kick again. Matthew tried to get it right. But the first time he wobbled and the second time he fell. He couldn't keep his balance.

"That does it," he said through gritted teeth. "Snakes can't kick. But I know something I can do." He thought about the answer sheet.

Tomorrow I'm going to get something right. Even if I have to do something wrong.

CHAPTER

EASY ANSWERS

Matthew overslept on Friday. Then the hot water ran out during his shower. Shivering, he ran to his bedroom.

The clock on his desk said 7:35. "I've got to hurry," Matthew said.

He dressed quickly. Then he grabbed his schoolbag and headed for the front door.

"Where are you going?" his mother called.

"I don't want to be late for school."

"Breakfast first," she said. "You have time."

Matthew dropped his schoolbag by the door and went to the breakfast table.

Mrs. Davis placed a bowl in front of him. "Eat first."

Matthew rolled his eyes. He wanted Cocoa-Loco cereal. The one with the crunchy chocolate bits, marshmallows, and a free prize. But today it was oatmeal.

"Why were you up so late last night?" his mother asked.

"How did you know?"

"Sitting under your blanket with a flashlight doesn't make you invisible." Mrs. Davis grinned. "Besides, you didn't invent that trick. What were you looking at?"

Matthew's hand went to his back pocket. The answer sheet was in there. "I was, uh, studying for the math test today," he said.

"Your father worked with you on your math all week. Did it help?"

"Kind of."

He ate fast. He didn't want to say they had *struggled* with fractions all week.

"I'm glad to see you're trying," his mother said. "You can do anything you want if you just work at it."

Matthew raised an eyebrow. "Can I stay home from school?" he asked.

"Don't push your luck," Mrs. Davis said. "We want you to make something of yourself."

"So you and Dad can be proud of me."

"More important than that," Mrs. Davis said. "So you can be proud of yourself."

Matthew felt as if the answer sheet were burning a hole in his pocket.

He crammed three spoonfuls of oatmeal into his mouth. "I'm finished," he mumbled and headed for the door.

"A good breakfast gets you through anything," Mrs. Davis said. "I'll see you when I get home from work." Mrs. Davis was a dispatcher at a taxi company. She told the drivers whom to pick up and where to take them.

"Your father will be home at his usual time." She opened the door for Matthew.

Mr. Davis worked for the post office. He had to be at work by 6:00 A.M.

"Okay, Mom," Matthew said. He picked up his

schoolbag, kissed her, and raced out the door.

He stopped when he hit the street. He took a deep breath and let it out. "Made it," he whispered.

The wind was blowing hard, but it wasn't cold. Matthew hurried along the street.

He had memorized almost all the test answers last night. He had only three more to go.

I don't get it, he thought as he reached the school building. Cheating was supposed to make things easier. But it didn't feel that way to him.

Matthew found an empty corner in the lunchroom and studied the answers.

When he saw Mr. Johnson arrive to pick up the class, Matthew ripped the answer sheet into tiny pieces. He dropped them in two different trash cans as he left the lunchroom.

Mr. Johnson handed out the tests as soon as the class was seated. The students got to work. All Matthew could hear was the scratching of pencils. He wrote down all the answers he'd memorized.

When Mr. Johnson collected the tests Matthew

buried his face in his hands. *I hope I got them right*, he prayed.

He looked up. Marissa was staring at him.

He knew what she was thinking. But it was too late now.

The day went by fast. He didn't speak to Marissa once.

Just before they were dismissed, Mr. Johnson said, "It didn't take me long to grade your tests."

"What did he do?" Matthew mumbled. "Skip lunch and his free period?"

"I did it during my lunch and free period," Mr. Johnson said.

"I'm pleased to say that most of you did very well." Mr. Johnson strolled up the aisle and placed Matthew's test in front of him. He smiled at Matthew. "Excellent work," he said.

A big 95 shone at the top of his test.

Marissa leaned over after Mr. Johnson passed by. "I hope you're satisfied," she said.

"I told you there wouldn't be any trouble."

"Not yet."

Matthew frowned. "What do you mean?" The bell rang. Marissa picked up her books and stormed out the door.

Matthew shrugged. "What does she know?" He picked up the test and stared at the 95.

Maybe all that work had been worth it after all.

Matthew grabbed his schoolbag and raced out of school. He couldn't wait to show his parents his high score!

CHAPTER

DOUBLE DISASTER

"I knew you could do it!" Mrs. Davis had been hugging and squeezing Matthew ever since she got home. "I told you."

"Right, Mom," Matthew said. He tried to wriggle free, but his mother wouldn't let go.

"I guess our studying together helped," said Mr. Davis.

Matthew nodded. *How much more of this do I have to take?* he wondered. "I'm glad you're glad," he told his parents. "May I go outside now?"

His parents glanced at each other. "Why not?" they said.

His mother gave him another hug. "You've earned a little fun time. But be back in an hour."

Matthew grabbed his jacket.

"This is only the beginning, son," said Mr. Davis.

Matthew stopped halfway out the door. "What do you mean, Dad?"

"Now that you know what it takes to get good grades," his father said, "we'll expect to see a lot more of them."

Matthew moaned.

"Oh, don't worry," his mother said. "We'll help you every step of the way."

Matthew closed the door and walked down stairs.

He wandered into the playground next to his building. He climbed to the top of the jungle gym and stared at the sky.

How was he going to get better grades all the time? He'd cheated to get this one.

* * *

The weekend didn't improve things. Matthew's parents didn't brag about the test. They just *happened* to mention it to almost everyone they spoke to.

When they weren't praising him, they were helping him with his homework.

It felt good to have their attention. It was easier to study with his parents' help.

But the more they praised him, the more uncomfortable he became.

He saw Marissa at church on Sunday. She saw him too. But she turned away from him.

Things got worse on Monday. At lunchtime, Matthew met Susan on her way to the cafeteria. She was wearing a T-shirt with a dinosaur on the front. It was crushing city buildings. The words on the shirt read: "I taught him everything he knows."

"I hear you used that new *study aid*," Susan said, louder than she had to. "It makes tests easy. Like you wrote them yourself."

"Not so loud," Matthew said. "You want everybody to hear? What's wrong with you and Marissa?"

"Did you know Marissa got a 66 on that test?"

Matthew shook his head.

"Guess we can't all be winners, can we?" Susan stalked off.

How much worse can things get? Matthew wondered. He found out later.

"After Friday's test," Mr. Johnson said, "I expect better work in class. Especially from certain people." Mr. Johnson smiled at Matthew.

Matthew hunched down in his seat. "Oh, brother," he moaned.

Math was still a foreign language to him. Friday's test had been too hard. He knew he would have failed without the answer sheet.

Matthew ducked his head. Maybe Mr. Johnson wouldn't call on him.

It didn't work.

Mr. Johnson called on Matthew more than ever. He gave the wrong answer each time. He could tell Mr. Johnson was surprised.

"Missing something?" Marissa whispered. "Maybe you need another *cheat sheet.*"

Tuesday was more of the same. By late afternoon, Mr. Johnson said, "You're back to your old standards. I had hoped you were finally improving."

Matthew looked down at his desk.

"Is there something I should know?"

"No, sir," Matthew said. "I'm just off a little."

Matthew knew he was in trouble. *I've got to talk to the gang at the dojo,* he told himself. *No matter what they think of me, they're my friends. And right now, I need all the friends I can get.*

CHAPTER

MR. 95

The gang was warming up when Matthew joined them.

"Look who's here," said Marissa. "It's Mr. 95."

"Look, I'm sorry about the test," he said. "I need help."

"What else is new?" Marissa said.

"You don't understand." Matthew told the kids about his parents' praising. "Then Mr. Johnson said I was back to my old standards."

"I knew you were going to get into trouble," Marissa said.

"And you were right!" Matthew said. "Now, how do I get out of it?"

Tommy called the class to order.

They walked to their rows.

"You have two choices," Jonathan said. "Either you tell everybody what happened. Or you let us dip you in boiling ski wax."

"I can't tell my folks," Matthew said.

"Then we'll get the ski wax ready."

Su walked into the room. She smiled and bowed to the class.

"Are you all right?" Susan asked.

Su smiled. "Thank you for asking about me," she said.

"What was the bad news you got?" Susan asked.

Su hesitated for a moment. "My brother was supposed to come here from Vietnam," she said. "He was going to live with Tommy and me. We've been planning this for some time."

"Su hasn't seen her brother in years," Tommy said.

Su's face grew sad. "But at the last minute, the government would not let him leave."

"Bummer," said Blair.

"I heard that people can sneak out of there," Matthew said. "Couldn't you lie about who he is and get him some phony ID?"

Su shook her head. "Many people sneak into this country. But then they must hide as if they were criminals. It's hard to build a new life living in the shadows."

"There's an old saying," Tommy said. "You cannot build a house on sand. It means you can't feel secure when the ground keeps shifting under you."

Matthew felt a knot in his stomach. Was that what he was doing by cheating?

"And lies are like sand," said Su. "I'll keep trying to find the honest way to bring my brother here. Until then, life goes on." She sat down on the floor. "Let's begin our preparation. Breathe."

Matthew found it easier to focus this time. He needed to be focused. As he calmed his mind, he saw that cheating was the same as lying.

At the end of class, Matthew told his friends what he was going to do.

"You're really going to tell your father?" Willy asked.

Matthew nodded.

"Matthew, your father's here," Tommy called from across the room.

"We'll come with you," Marissa said.

"Thanks," said Matthew. "But don't stand too close. I don't want you caught in the blast when he explodes."

With his head down, Matthew walked over to his father. Tommy was standing next to Mr. Davis.

"Dad, there's something I have to tell you." Susan, Willy, and Jonathan stood behind Matthew. Marissa stood next to him. Matthew explained how he had cheated on the math test. Then he told his father everything that had happened since.

Mr. Davis and Tommy listened carefully.

"The gang here, and something Su and Tommy told me . . . " Matthew paused. "Well, they made me see I wasn't feeling any better because of my 95. I felt worse."

"Why?" Mr. Davis asked.

"Because I felt like a phony."

"He's a jerk," Marissa said.

"And he wants people to think he's too cool for words," Susan added.

"But he's really a good guy," said Willy.

Jonathan stepped forward. "Please don't cream him, Mr. Davis."

"And please don't take him out of karate school," Marissa said.

"His mother and I have to talk about this," Mr. Davis told them. "That's all I can say for now."

"I'd be glad to help in any way I can," Tommy told Mr. Davis. "If you want to talk."

"Thank you," Mr. Davis replied. "I'll think about it. Come on, Matthew."

Matthew glanced at Tommy and his friends. Then he followed his father out of the dojo.

As he walked down the front steps, he was sure he'd never see the Cool Karate School again.

C H A P T E R

THE RIGHT
CHOICE

rs. Davis listened to Matthew in silence.

"Are you real mad with me?" Matthew asked her.

His mother cleared her throat twice before she spoke. Her voice trembled and she didn't look at him. "I'm . . . terribly . . . disappointed in you," she said. "You really let me down, Matthew."

Mr. Davis sent Matthew to his room. Later, Mr. Davis told Matthew they would go to school with him tomorrow afternoon. And it would be up to Matthew to confess.

Matthew had expected his parents to be angry. Or embarrassed. He never expected them to be hurt.

This really stinks, he thought. *I blew it*. His eyes began to sting. A few seconds later, tears rolled down his cheeks.

* * *

The next day, Matthew sat in the principal's office with his parents and Mr. Johnson. He told his story.

"Why did you choose to tell us now?" Mr. Polanski asked.

"I'm not sure," Matthew replied. "I did something wrong. And it made me feel bad afterward. That's it, I guess."

"I see," said the principal.

"And . . . " Matthew hesitated. "You can't build a house on sand."

Mr. Polanski and Mr. Johnson exchanged looks.

"That's something he learned in his karate class," his father explained.

Mr. Polanski leaned across his desk. "And what action should I take in this matter?"

Matthew shrank into the chair. "I don't know, sir."

Mr. Polanski looked up at Mr. and Mrs. Davis. "Well, I think we do." Mr. Johnson nodded.

Matthew swallowed hard.

* * *

An elevated train rumbled overhead as Matthew and his parents walked down the street. The wind whipped papers and leaves along the sidewalk.

When they reached the karate school, Matthew saw the gang.

"We weren't sure you'd come," said Willy.

"I saw you go into Mr. Polanski's office with your parents," Susan said.

"And you didn't come back to class afterward," said Marissa. "We thought—"

"No, he hasn't been expelled," said Mrs. Davis.

"But he did have to take the test again," said his father.

"It was brutal," Matthew groaned. "I'll have to stay after school twice a week for extra study time."

"Mr. Johnson volunteered to work with him," Mrs. Davis said.

"Plus, I'm grounded for life, or a million light-years. Whichever comes first."

"Does that mean you're going to yank him out of karate school?" Jonathan asked.

"No," said Mr. Davis. "What he learned here helped him make the right choice."

"He finally did something right!" Marissa grinned.

Matthew thought he saw his mother smile. But it vanished. "We decided he can keep karate," she said. "And Tommy and Su have offered to help in any way they can. Matthew is learning more here than just breaking bricks and boards."

"So he can go to class?" Willy asked.

"Yes, he can," Mrs. Davis said.

Matthew and his friends began to cheer, "Snake, Dragon, Tiger, Leopard, Crane! Karate, karate! We've done it again!"

They slapped high fives and raced into the dojo. But Matthew stopped at the doors and looked back at his parents.

He thought about how Su was willing to do

things the right way. Even if it meant she wouldn't see her brother for a long time.

Matthew was glad he and his family were together.

He knew he'd probably still fool around in school, a little. He was still the Snake. But he would never let his parents down like that again.

He gave his mother a hug.

"Go get 'em, Snake," said Mr. Davis.

Matthew grinned and raced into the dojo.

This is Steve DeMasco, creator of the Cool Karate School books, and five of his students.

Steve has a seventh-degree black belt in karate. That means he's one of the best karate experts in the world. He has appeared in movies and is the star of a self-defense videotape.

Steve believes kids can learn good values from karate—and have a lot of fun too.

These kids are just starting out, but they're doing great. They really get a kick out of karate—just like the kids of the Cool Karate School!